STARTING OUT

baby
PANDAS

KATE RIGGS

CREATIVE EDUCATION • CREATIVE PAPERBACKS

...ENTS

I Am a Cub   4

Clean and Warm   6

On the Move   8

I Am a Young Panda   10

Speak and Listen   12

Cub Words   14

Reading Corner   15

Index   16

I AM A CUB.

I am a baby panda.

ear

paw

nose

4

I was born in a <u>den</u>.
I was as small as a
stick of butter!

My mother licked my pink skin clean. She kept me warm.

I can stand and walk at 10 weeks old. My coat is getting thick and fluffy.

I am hungry all the time! I drink my mother's milk. Soon my baby teeth come in.

Now I can eat bamboo. At one year old, my second set of teeth grows in.

I am a young panda!

SPEAK AND LISTEN

MMMEEE

EEEEEE!

Can you speak like a cub?
Pandas squeal, squeak,
and grunt.

Listen to these sounds:

https://www.youtube.com
/watch?v=Oi_umBoKNp8

Now it is
your turn!

CUB WORDS

bamboo: a fast-growing, woody grass

den: a small, hidden area where an animal rests

READING CORNER

Olson, Bethany. *Baby Pandas.*
Minneapolis: Bellwether Media, 2014.

Sirota, Lyn A. *Giant Pandas*. North
Mankato, Minn.: Capstone Press, 2010.

Trueit, Trudi Strain. *Giant Pandas*.
North Mankato, Minn.: Amicus, 2016.

INDEX

coats 8

dens 6

ears 5

family 7, 10

food 10, 11

movement 8, 9

noses 5

size 6

sounds 13

teeth 10, 11

PUBLISHED BY CREATIVE EDUCATION AND CREATIVE PAPERBACKS
P.O. Box 227, Mankato, Minnesota 56002
Creative Education and Creative Paperbacks
are imprints of The Creative Company
www.thecreativecompany.us

LIBRARY OF CONGRESS CATALOGING-IN-PUBLICATION DATA
Names: Riggs, Kate, author.
Title: Baby pandas / Kate Riggs.
Series: Starting out.
Summary: A baby panda narrates the story of its life, describing how physical features, diet, habitat, and familial relationships play a role in its growth and development.

Identifiers: ISBN 978-1-64026-250-8 (hardcover)
ISBN 978-1-62832-813-4 (pbk)
ISBN 978-1-64000-391-0 (eBook)
This title has been submitted for CIP processing
under LCCN 2019938710.

CCSS: RI.K.1, 2, 3, 4, 5, 6, 7; RI.1.1, 2, 3, 4, 5, 6, 7;
RF.K.1, 3; RF.1.1

DESIGN AND PRODUCTION
by Chelsey Luther and Joe Kahnke
Art direction by Rita Marshall
Printed in the United States of America

PHOTOGRAPHS by Alamy (National Geographic Image Collection, ZUMA Press, Inc.), Getty Images (China Photos/Stringer/Getty Images News, VCG), iStockphoto (GlobalP), Minden Pictures (Katherine Feng, Andy Rouse), National Geographic Creative (Joel Sartore/National Geographic Photo Ark), Shutterstock (Bohbeh, dang-dumrong, Eric Isselee)

FIRST EDITION HC 9 8 7 6 5 4 3 2 1
FIRST EDITION PBK 9 8 7 6 5 4 3 2 1